ON THE TRAIL

Can you match the muddy footprints with the animals that made them?

Answer on page 47.

3

ALL THE LIVELONG DAY

We've been working on the railroad! To find all the railroad words hidden in this engine, look across, down, up, backward, and diagonally. Keep on track, though, because the leftover letters will spell out the first line of a famous folk song.

AIR BRAKE	CROSSING	LOCOMOTIVE
AXLE	DRAWBAR	MAIL
BEND	ENGINE	RAIL
BOXCAR	ENGINEER	SCHEDULE
CABOOSE	GANDY DANCER	SIDING
CHUG	GATES	SMOKE
CLANG	GAUGE	SPIKES
COAL	GONDOLA	TIES
CONDUCTOR	HISS	TRACKS
COUPLER	HOBO	WHISTLE
COWCATCHER	LINES	YARD

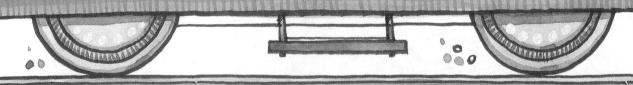

Illustrated by Jeffrey Stahler

WHAT'S NEXT?

Can you draw in what figure comes next in each row?

1.

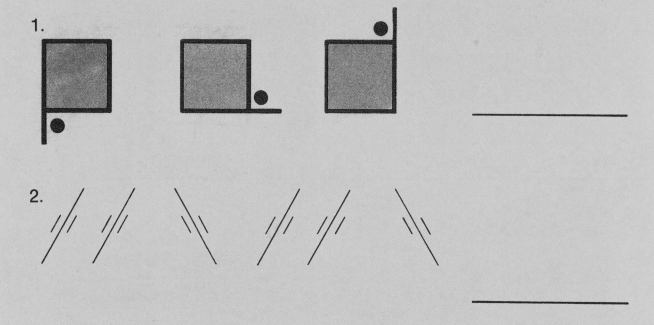

2.

3.

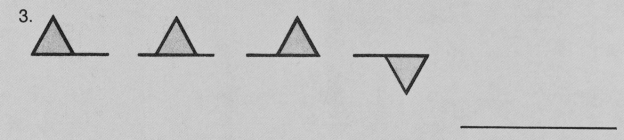

4.

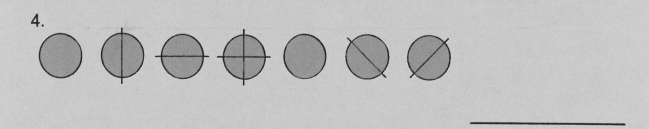

5.

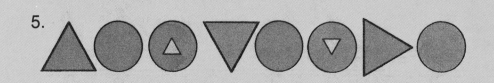

Illustrated by Rob Sepanak

Answer on page 47.

IN SO MANY WORDS

Unscramble the first set of letters below four times to make
four different words. Each letter will be used only once in
each word. The clues will help you sort out the choices.

A E L P T

__ __ __ __ __   1. A dish

__ __ __ __ __   2. A fold sewn into a skirt

__ __ __ __ __   3. Jumped

__ __ __ __ __   4. Part of a flower

Now try these letters to make six new words.

O P S T

__ __ __ __   1. Don't go

__ __ __ __   2. Spinning toys

__ __ __ __   3. Cooking vessels

__ __ __ __   4. To mail something

__ __ __ __   5. Chooses

__ __ __ __   6. Good name for a dog

Answer on page 47.

DOUBLE UP

Almost all the things pictured here contain double letters in their names. For example, there's an OTTER and a LADDER. Look and see how many other words with double letters you can find. Hurry, and find them on the double.

Illustrated by Gregg Valley

ROW, ROW, ROW

Each of these scarecrows has something in common with the two others in the same row. For example, all three scarecrows in the top row across are wearing red hats. Look at the other rows across, down, and diagonally. What's alike in each row?

Illustrated by John Nez

Answer on page 47.

TO THE CONTRARY

Mary, Mary, quite contrary, what is she growing now? Could it be prize petunias or a gigantic beanstalk? A shoetree for her slippers or a plant that can iron wrinkled sheets? Use your imagination to draw what you think is growing out of Mary's flower pot.

MANSION OF MYSTERY

Many treasure hunters have tried to spend a night in the spooky old King mansion, searching for the vast fortune hidden inside. Starting at the front door, see if you can follow the directions and gather the letters in the proper sequence. These will lead you to the treasure, and will tell you what is hidden in the locked trunk.

1. Before going in, take the letter from the door knocker. Now look for the grandfather clock.
2. Take the letter from the clock. Head upstairs to the red room.
3. You want the letter on the pillows. Now get something to eat.
4. Open the refrigerator slowly for the next letter. Head into the garden.
5. The letter you're after is growing from that mound. Go up the kitchen stairs.
6. Along the way, pull the letter from the second painting.
7. In the attic, the spiders have the letter you want.
8. Outside on the roof is where the next letter is shining. Be careful!
9. Back inside, the library has the next letter you need. Take the yellow one.
10. As you pull that letter, a secret panel swings open to reveal the treasure. Look straight in to find the last letter.
11. To uncover what's in the waiting chest, take the letters you've collected and read them backwards.

Answer on page 47.

RHYME TIME

All the opposites of the words below rhyme with one another. Do you know what all the opposites are?

1. Hot _____

2. Young _____

3. Shy _____

4. Soothe _____

5. Unpleat _____

6. Release _____

7. Kept secret _____

8. Free form _____

9. Available _____

10. Flattened _____

Answer on page 47.

Illustrated by Barbara Gray

SPY GUY

Can you sneak past this top spy by finding a path from start to finish?

START

FINISH

FOND OF PONDS

Ponds can be busy places. All the words listed below are things that can be found in or around a pond. Use the number of letters as clues to figure out where each word fits in the graph on the next page. It may help to cross each word off the list as you use it. Now get hopping!

Answer on page 48.

Illustrated by Barbara Gray

4 LETTERS

CROW	MICE
DEER	POOL
DUCK	REED
EGGS	SWAN
FISH	TOAD
LAKE	

3 LETTERS

BAT	MUD
BEE	OAK
ICE	OWL

5 LETTERS

ALGAE	HERON	SWAMP
BEARS	ROCKS	TREES
GEESE	SKUNK	WASPS
GREEN	SNAIL	WEEDS
	SNAKE	

6 LETTERS

BEETLE	SPIDER
GREBES	STREAM
HORNET	TURTLE
MINNOW	WILLOW

8 LETTERS

BLOSSOMS	MOSQUITO
BULLFROG	POLLIWOG
CATTAILS	SONGBIRD
LILY PADS	WATER BUG
MILKWEED	

9 LETTERS

BUTTERFLY
DRAGONFLY
WATER LILY

7 LETTERS

RACCOON
TADPOLE

10 LETTERS

FIELD MOUSE
SALAMANDER

11 LETTERS

WILDFLOWERS

AS YOU LIKE IT

Three girls have prepared a list of their likes and dislikes. Can you figure out how each girl decides whether or not she likes something? Each girl likes her own name and each has a different reason for why she likes something.

Kay

Likes:
- Tea
- Eyes
- Why
- Jays
- You

Dislikes:
- Coffee
- Noses
- Where
- Crows
- Them

Viola

Likes:
- Hornets
- Drumsticks
- Cellophane
- Harpoons
- Organdy

Dislikes:
- Bumblebees
- Wings
- Wax paper
- Bayonets
- Silk

Megan

Likes:
- Italy
- Weeks
- Heroes
- Sheep
- Young

Dislikes:
- France
- Days
- Villains
- Lambs
- Old

Illustrated by Terry Rogers

Answer on page 48.

SWIMMING MEMORIES

Take a long look at this picture. Try to remember everything you see in it. Then turn the page, and try to answer some questions about it without looking back.

Illustrated by John Nez

DON'T READ THIS UNTIL YOU HAVE LOOKED AT "Swimming Memories—Part 1" ON PAGE 19

SWIMMING MEMORIES   Part 2

Can you answer these questions about the swimming scene you saw? Don't peek!

1. What color bathing suit was the instructor wearing?
2. What was around the instructor's neck?
3. What design was on the ship's flag?
4. Which way was the wind blowing?
5. How many girls were in the class?
6. What kind of boat was tied to the dock?
7. What wasn't allowed in this class?
8. What stroke were the swimmers practicing?
9. What animals were watching?
10. Was this fresh water or salt water?

Answer on page 48.

21

Each number from 3 through 11 can be placed into one of these squares so that each row will add up to 21. The rows go across, down, and diagonally. 6 and 8 are already in place to get you started.

Illustrated by Rob Sepanak

Answer on page 48.

GRID LOCK

Don't get locked out. Use the clues below to fill in this grid.

Across

1. Entire
4. Foot wear
6. Measure of land
8. Chuckle; giggle
9. Abbreviation for "right turn"
10. Abbreviation for "background"
11. A room at the top of a house
13. Rinse
14. Current events
16. Paid out money

Down

1. Warm product that comes from sheep
2. The Wizard's country
3. Apiece
4. Thin tube for sipping drinks
5. Our planet
6. Once more
7. Rims
11. Inquires
12. Penny
15. Not you

PICTURE MIXER

Copy these mixed-up squares in the spaces on the next page to put this picture back together. The letters and numbers tell you where each square belongs. The first one, A-3, has been done for you.

Illustrated by Rob Sepanak

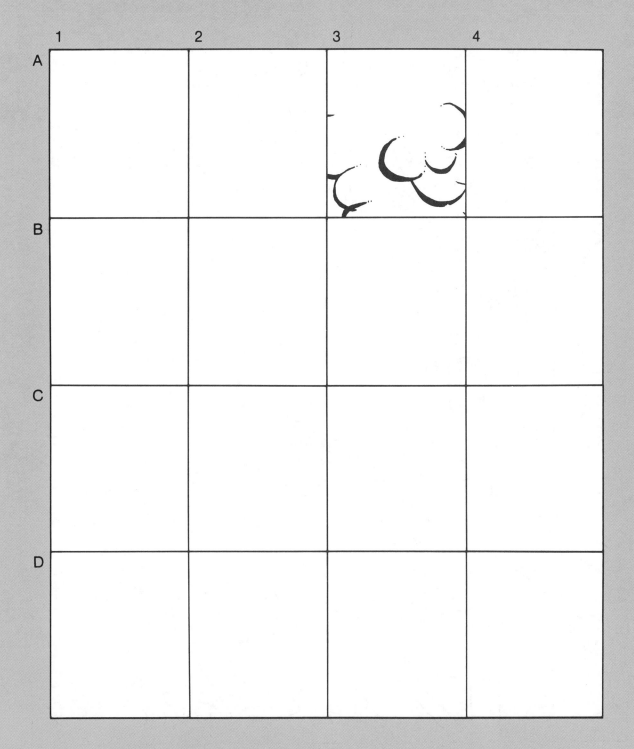

VERY VISUAL

A chevron is a shape that looks like a wedge or a big V.
How many chevrons can you find on this page?

Illustrated by R. Michael Palan

INVESTIG-"ATION"

The clues below give you information about words that end in "ation." Can you name the "ation" that . . .

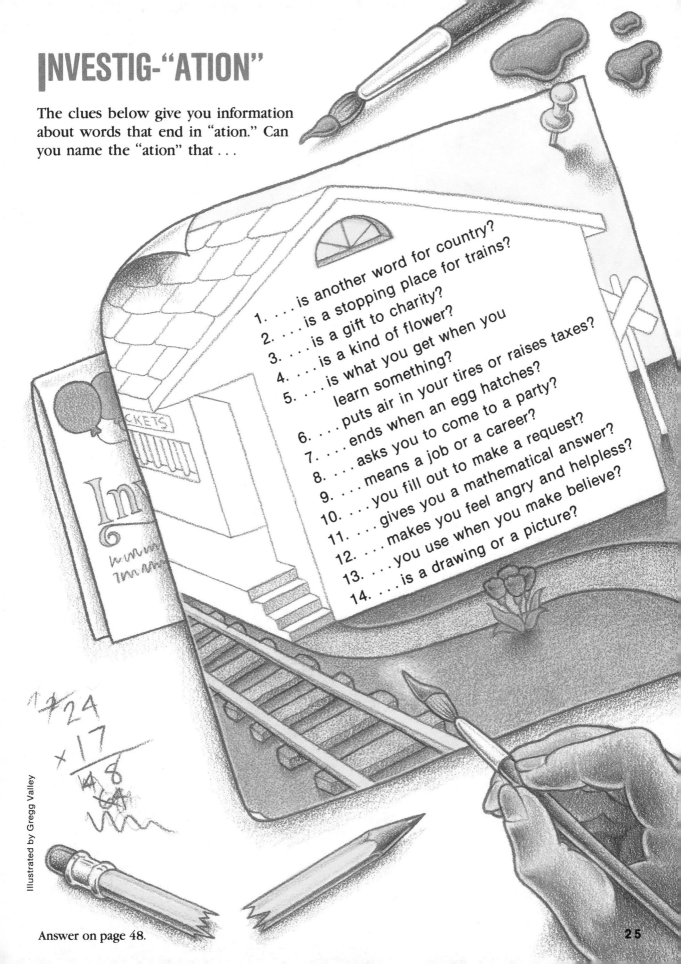

1. . . . is another word for country?
2. . . . is a stopping place for trains?
3. . . . is a gift to charity?
4. . . . is a kind of flower?
5. . . . is what you get when you learn something?
6. . . . puts air in your tires or raises taxes?
7. . . . ends when an egg hatches?
8. . . . asks you to come to a party?
9. . . . means a job or a career?
10. . . . you fill out to make a request?
11. . . . gives you a mathematical answer?
12. . . . makes you feel angry and helpless?
13. . . . you use when you make believe?
14. . . . is a drawing or a picture?

Illustrated by Gregg Valley

Answer on page 48.

MONKEY BUSINESS

In their rush to grab these bananas, the monkeys have gotten their vines all tangled. Can you follow each vine to see what monkey will get which bananas?

Answer on page 48.

Illustrated by Lynn Adams

STOP, LOOK, AND LIST

Under each category, list one thing that begins with each letter. For example, one thing that flies that begins with "C" is Canary. See if you can name another.

THINGS THAT FLY

C _____

R _____

B _____

P _____

S _____

TYPES OF BREADS OR ROLLS

C _____

R _____

B _____

P _____

S _____

BODIES OF WATER

C _____

R _____

B _____

P _____

S _____

Illustrated by Lisa Dayer

Answer on page 49.

HIDDEN PICTURES

There are at least 22 objects hidden on these pages.
How many can you find?

OUT TO THE BALL GAME

How many differences can you see between these two pictures?

DOT MAGIC

Connect the dots to find out who is always "in the pink."

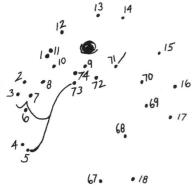

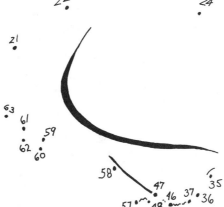
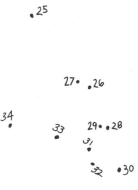

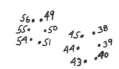
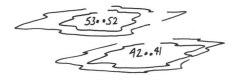

Illustrated by Rob Sepanak

THE DANCING MEN

Secret codes have been around a long time. The one on this page is over 100 years old. It first appeared in a Sherlock Holmes story called "The Adventure of the Dancing Men."

On the next page is a message that Dr. Watson probably never sent to Sherlock Holmes. Use the chart below to help you figure out the riddle. Letters marked with a small flag show the end of a word.

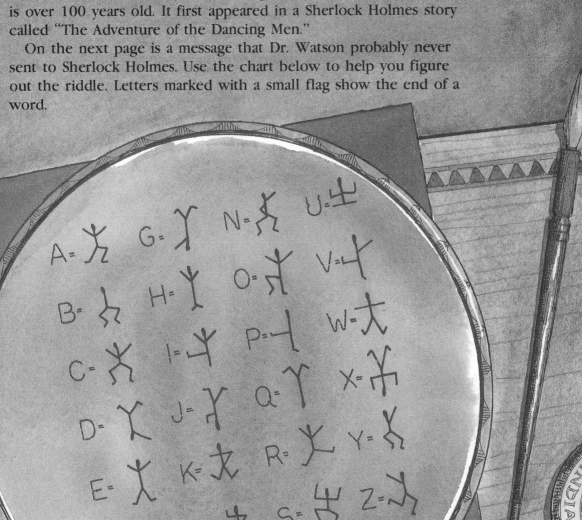

Answer on page 49.

Illustrated by Anni Matsick

TRUCK TROUBLE

How many things can you find wrong in this parade?

PLUS PATH

To find your way through this maze, add the first pair of numbers (5+2). Draw a line to the answer (7), then move ahead to the next pair of numbers and do the same. Answers may be to the left, right, up or down.

INCREDIBLE EDIBLES

Many foods have foreign nationalities as part of their names. Using the map as a clue, can you identify each of the nationalities which lends extra flavor to the food listed here? One has been done to give you a taste.

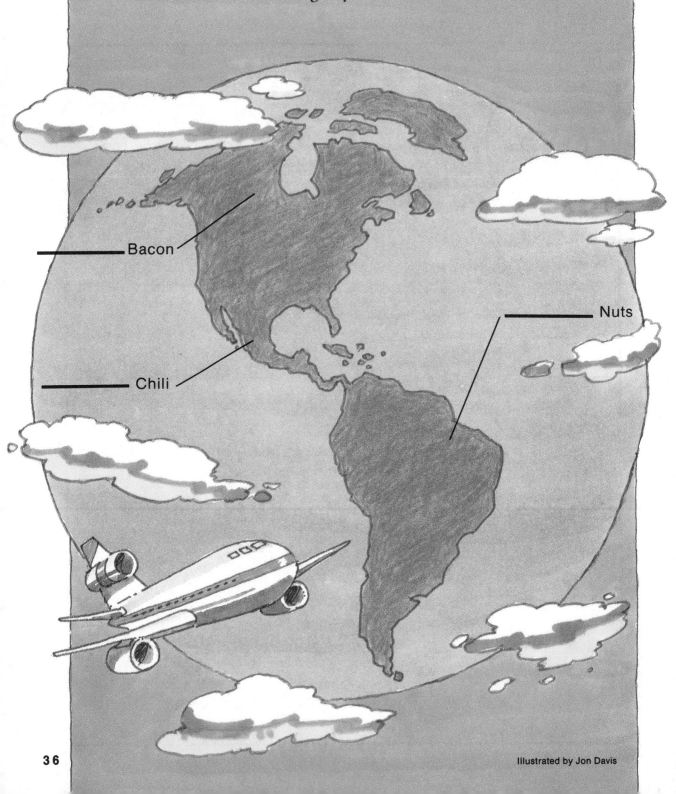

Bacon

Nuts

Chili

Illustrated by Jon Davis

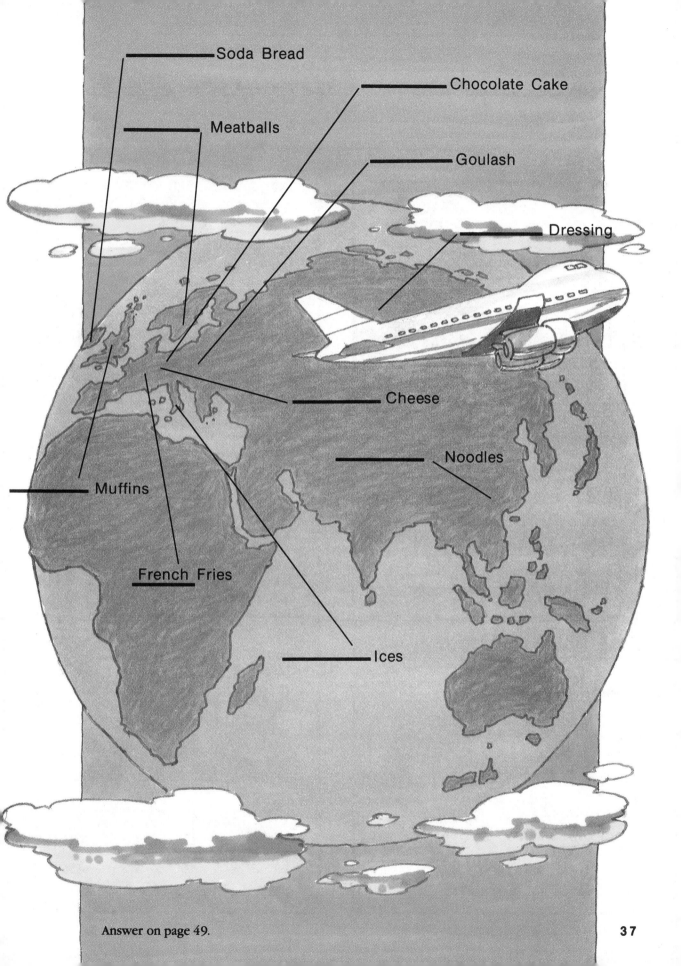

Soda Bread

Chocolate Cake

Meatballs

Goulash

Dressing

Cheese

Noodles

Muffins

French Fries

Ices

FLIGHT PLANS

These are some scenes of Kerry and Kelly's first sky diving flight. Can you put the pictures in order to show what the plane did first, second, and so on?

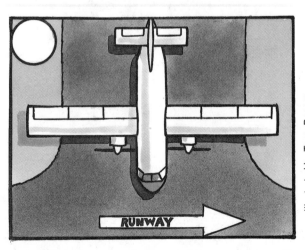

Illustrated by Terry Rogers

Answer on page 49.

INSTANT PICTURE

Hidden on this page is something you would never ride in a race.
To find out if it fits your hobby, fill in all the spaces that have two dots.

Illustrated by Rob Sepanak

THE CASE OF THE LONESOME LADYBUG

See if you can solve this mystery. Read the story and fill in the
missing words. Then match the numbered letters with the
corresponding spaces at the end of the story. If you've filled in the
spaces correctly, you'll find out what happened to the ladybug's friend.

Lucy Ladybug and Carrie Caterpillar were very best __ __ __ __ __ __ __ .
                                                      8

They liked to crawl together up the thick, rough __ __ __ __ __ of the big
                                                  14   9

elm __ __ __ __ and to play among its rustling __ __ __ __ __ __ .
    6   18

Sometimes they had to hide from the robins and other __ __ __ __ __
                                                      2

that perched on the swaying __ __ __ __ __ __ __ __ . Every morning
                            11

they watched the __ __ __ rise in the east, and every evening they watched
                 5

it set in the __ __ __ __
              15

One day, however, Carrie __ __ __ __ Lucy that she had to go away for
                         13

a while. "I have very important things to do," she said. "But I promise to

come back as soon as possible."

Lucy said a sad __ __ __ __ __ __ __ to her friend, and Carrie crawled
                                    19

slowly out onto a branch and disappeared among the leaves.

Illustrated by Judith Hunt

As the days went by, Lucy missed Carrie so much. To pass the time, she

watched big bumblebees as they searched for ___ ___ ___ ___ ___ ___ among
                                                              3

the brightly colored ___ ___ ___ ___ ___ ___ ___ , and she followed the little
                          17

garter ___ ___ ___ ___ ___ as it glided through the blades of ___ ___ ___ ___ ___ .
            4   16

Even so, she didn't have much ___ ___ ___ without her friend, Carrie
                                        12

___ ___ ___ ___ ___ ___ ___ ___ ___ ___ ___ .
                    10

   Finally, after several weeks, Lucy decided that Carrie was not coming back.

She was so ___ ___ ___ that she cried.
                1

   "I have lost my good friend," she wailed.

   At that moment, she heard a familiar ___ ___ ___ ___ ___ behind her. "No,
                                                  7

you haven't," it said. "I've come back, just as I promised."

   Lucy turned, and gasped with amazement at what she saw.

What did Lucy see when she turned around?

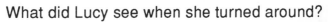

___ ___ ___ ___ ___ ___ ___ ___ ___ ___ ___ ___ ___ ___ ___ ___ ___ ___ ___
 1   2   3   4   5   6   7   8   9   10   11   12   13   14   15   16   17   18   19

WANDA'S WALLPAPER

Which wallpaper does Wanda want? Wanda doesn't want anything blue unless it's a triangle. She doesn't want flowers or stripes. She *does* want it to go with her red furniture.

1

2

3

4

5

6

7
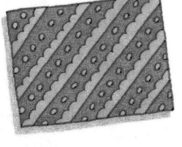

8

9

Illustrated by Barbara Gray

Answer on page 50.

WHAT'S IN A WORD?

A VETERINARIAN is a doctor to go to when your pet is sick. But let's go to this VETERINARIAN to get over 40 words of three letters or more. EAR and NERVE are two of the words you might find. How many other words can you make from the letters in VETERINARIAN?

Illustrated by Lynn Adams

Answer on page 50.

UNEASY RIDERS

If you look carefully, you may be able to spot the two bicycle riders that are exactly the same.

Illustrated by R. Michael Palan

LETTER DROP

Only six of the letters in the top line will work through this maze to land in the numbered squares at the bottom. When they get there, they will spell out something to share with your friends.

U.S. MAIL

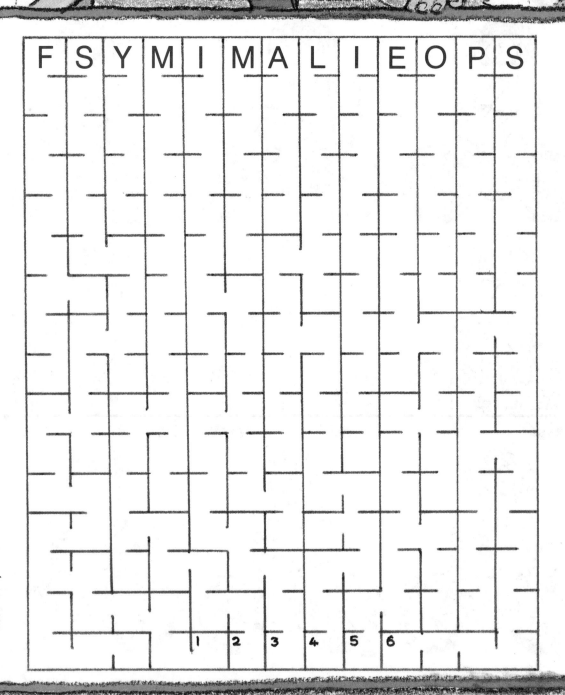

F S Y M I M A L I E O P S

1 2 3 4 5 6

Answer on page 50.

ANSWERS

ON THE TRAIL (page 3)

ALL THE LIVELONG DAY (pages 4-5)

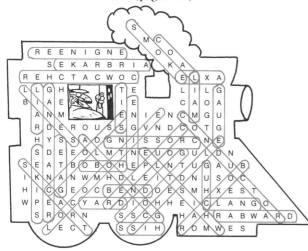

The leftover letters say: She'll be coming 'round the mountain when she comes, when she comes.

WHAT'S NEXT? (page 6)

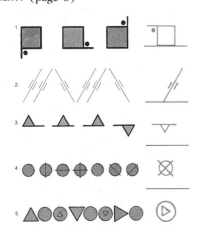

IN SO MANY WORDS (page 7)

1. PLATE
2. PLEAT
3. LEAPT
4. PETAL

1. STOP
2. TOPS
3. POTS
4. POST
5. OPTS
6. SPOT

ROW, ROW, ROW (page 10)

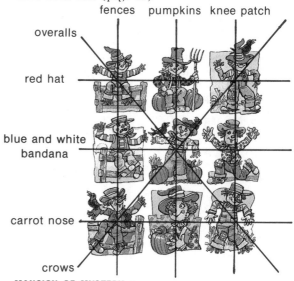

overalls — fences   pumpkins   knee patch
red hat
blue and white bandana
carrot nose
crows

MANSION OF MYSTERY (pages 12-13)
You've found COMIC BOOKS.

RHYME TIME (page 14)

1. cold
2. old
3. bold
4. scold
5. fold
6. hold
7. told
8. mold
9. sold
10. rolled

SPY GUY (page 15)

FOND OF PONDS (pages 16-17)

AS YOU LIKE IT (page 18)

Kay likes things that sound like letters of the alphabet.
Viola likes things that begin with the name of a musical instrument (*horn*ets).
Megan likes things that begin with a pronoun (*It*aly).

SWIMMING MEMORIES (page 20)

1. Blue
2. A key on a necklace
3. An anchor
4. Right to left
5. Two
6. A rubber raft
7. Diving
8. The backstroke
9. A dolphin and a dog
10. Most likely salt, due to the dolphin and the lighthouse

21 (page 20)

GRID LOCK (page 21)

PICTURE MIXER (pages 22-23)

INVESTIG-"ATION" (page 25)

1. nation
2. station
3. donation
4. carnation
5. education
6. inflation
7. incubation
8. invitation
9. occupation
10. application
11. calculation
12. frustration
13. imagination
14. illustration

MONKEY BUSINESS (page 26)

STOP, LOOK, AND LIST (page 27)
Here are our answers. You may have found others.

Things That Fly
Crow
Rocket
Balloon
Plane
Sparrow

Types of Breads or Rolls
Croissant
Rye
Bagel
Pumpernickel
Sesame

Bodies of Water
Canal
River
Brook
Pond
Sea

DOT MAGIC (page 31)

THE DANCING MEN (pages 32-33)
What is the biggest potato in the world?
A hip-potato-mus.

PLUS PATH (page 35)

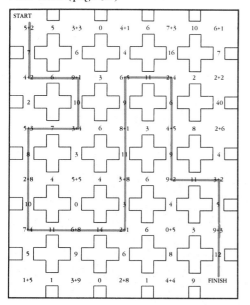

INCREDIBLE EDIBLES (pages 36-37)
Canadian Bacon
Mexican Chili
Irish Soda Bread
English Muffins
French Fries
German Chocolate Cake
Russian Dressing
Swiss Cheese
Swedish Meatballs
Hungarian Goulash
Italian Ices
Chinese Noodles
Brazil Nuts

FLIGHT PLANS (page 38)
3   1
6   5
4   2

INSTANT PICTURE (page 39)

THE CASE OF THE LONESOME LADYBUG (pages 40-41)
Lucy Ladybug and Carrie Caterpillar were very best FRIENDS. They liked to crawl together up the thick, rough TRUNK of the big elm TREE and to play among its rustling LEAVES. Sometimes they had to hide from the robins and other BIRDS that perched on the swaying BRANCHES. Every morning they watched the SUN rise in the east, and every evening they watched it set in the WEST.

One day, however, Carrie TOLD Lucy that she had to go away for a while. "I have very important things to do," she said. "But I promise to come back as soon as possible."

Lucy said a sad GOODBYE to her friend. Carrie crawled slowly out onto a branch and disappeared among the leaves.

As the days went by, Lucy missed Carrie very much. To pass the time, she watched the big bumble-bees as they searched for POLLEN among the brightly colored FLOWERS, and she followed the little garter SNAKE as it glided through the blades of GRASS. Still, she didn't have much FUN without her friend, Carrie CATERPILLAR.

Finally, after several weeks, Lucy decided that Carrie was not coming back. She was so SAD that she cried.

"I have lost my good friend," Lucy wailed.

At that moment, she heard a familiar VOICE behind her. "No, you haven't," it said. "I've come back, just as I promised."

Lucy turned, and she gasped with amazement at what she saw.

What did Lucy see when she turned around?

A BEAUTIFUL BUTTERFLY
1 2 3 4 5 6 7 8 9 10 11 12 13 14 15 16 17 18 19

WANDA'S WALLPAPER (page 42)
Wanda wants wallpaper number one.

WHAT'S IN A WORD? (page 43)
Here are the words we found. You may have found others.

air	naïve	ten
ant	native	terrain
art	near	tie
avert	neat	tin
earn	net	tire
eat	rain	train
enter	rat	tree
era	rave	trivia
err	raven	van
event	rear	vat
inert	rent	veer
intern	rite	vein
invent	tan	vent
Iran	tar	via
irate	tear	vine

UNEASY RIDERS (pages 44-45)

LETTER DROP (page 46)
SMILES

Editor: Jeffrey A. O'Hare • **Art Director:** Timothy J. Gillner
Project Director: Pamela Gallo • **Editorial Consultant:** Andrew Gutelle
Design Consultant: Bob Feldgus

Puzzle Contributors
George Anderson • Barbara Backer • Mary Marks Cezus • Debra Cole
Jeanette C. Grote • Elaine Hilowitz • Eleanor Klein • Shirley Marshall
Teresa Lynn Morningstar • Jan Onffroy • Arline Rose • Donna Siple
Bernard Traciak • Marjon Van Oort • Jabeen Yusufali